Acknowledgment

The Bible passages on the endpapers are from The Good News Bible, *published by the Bible Societies and Collins,* © *American Bible Society 1976.*
   Used by permission.

First edition

The Miracles of Jesus
The loaves and fishes

retold for easy reading
by SYLVIA MANDEVILLE
illustrated by ROGER HALL

Ladybird Books Loughborough

THE LOAVES AND FISHES

Something woke Jonathan up. It was the sound of a boat being dragged down to the water.

Jonathan peered over the edge of his father's fishing boat, where he had fallen asleep in the hot afternoon sun.

Some men were launching a boat. "You are very tired," one of them was saying. "We'll row over to a quiet spot, then you can have a rest, and tell us all about your travels."

Jonathan settled back on to a pile of dry nets, to sleep again.

Just as he had made himself comfortable, more voices caught his attention.

"There He is! He's gone out in a boat with His disciples."

"Come on," said another voice, "let's run round the edge of the lake to meet Him when He lands."

Suddenly the beach was full of men, women and children, running and calling out to each other, "This way to find Jesus."

Jonathan jumped from his boat. So that was Jesus rowing off with His friends! Jonathan wanted to see Him too. He grabbed his basket of food and hurried off with the crowd.

"My father's bad leg was healed by Jesus last week," a woman was saying.

"I want Him to heal my swollen arm today."

"He cured my son's fever," a man said as they ran, puffing and panting round the shore.

There were so many people that Jonathan was almost crushed in the crowd.

"There's the boat. There He is!" a man called. "It's coming in just up there in the bay."

Jonathan was quite out of breath, but he ran on.

They arrived at the water's edge just in time to steady the boat as Jesus stepped out.

Jesus looked into their eyes. He saw the suffering of those who were ill.

"They are like poor sheep with no shepherd," He said to His disciples.

He walked in amongst the crowd,
putting His hands gently on the sick, the
deaf and the blind, healing each one of
them.

Then He began to tell stories, and
everyone settled down to listen to Him.

He told stories about mustard seeds,
fishes, nets, hidden treasure and pearls,
– all to do with the Kingdom of God.
Jonathan listened intently.

Time passed and the sun sank lower
in the sky.

14

As Jesus ended His teaching, one of His disciples said to Him, "This is a very lonely place, Jesus. It is getting late and the people are a long way from their homes. They are hungry now, and tired. Send them away before it gets dark. Send them into the villages to buy food."

Jonathan had been leaning on a rock close to Jesus all this time, hearing every word that was said.

"The crowd need not go away. Give them something to eat," Jesus said.

"Has anyone brought any food?" the disciples called out to the crowd.

"We ran here in a hurry. We didn't think about food," everyone answered – except for Jonathan, who held up his basket. Andrew, one of Jesus' disciples, led him over to Jesus.

"This boy has got some food," he said, and he unpacked the basket.

"He has five barley loaves and two small fishes. What good is that amongst such a big crowd?"

Jesus picked up the crisp brown bread and the two fishes.

Jonathan smiled at Jesus. He wanted to say, "I don't mind if you eat them all," but he was too shy.

"Tell everyone to sit down, in groups of fifty," Jesus said to His disciples.

As people sat down, their clothes spread out round them, making a bright pattern of colour.

Jesus stood with the food in His hands. He looked up to the sky and thanked God for it.

Then He broke up the barley loaves and the two small fishes. He handed it out to the disciples.

"Share this among the people," He

said. The disciples went round to every group. Jonathan got some. The family by him got some. The men behind him got some. Every single person in every group got some.

"I feel quite full," said Jonathan, ʾping his mouth.

"How many people do you think are here?" Jonathan asked a neighbour when he had finished eating.

"I've been doing a quick count, and judging by the number of groups, I should reckon well over five thousand," answered the neighbour. "Five thousand men that is, not counting women and children."

"Over five thousand!" said Jonathan, amazed. "And they've all eaten my dinner!"

Then he called out suddenly, "I'll help!" The disciples were coming round again with big baskets, picking up all the crusts and crumbs which the people had dropped.

Soon, twelve baskets were full, and nothing was wasted.

The men began to talk to each other.

"We could do with a man like Jesus to be our king," one of them said.

"Yes," said another. "If He can feed us like this every day, and heal us when we are ill, He would make a good king."

"Come on," said another. "Let's go and make Him our king."

Jesus knew what the men were thinking. He called His disciples to Him. "You go on ahead of me in the boat, back to the other side. I want to be quiet here for a while, by myself," He said.

"And all of you," He said to the crowds, "go back safely now to your homes."

Jonathan joined a family he knew for the long walk home.

"Wait until I tell my mother how many people ate my dinner!" he said.

And as they left, Jesus climbed higher up the mountain to pray, so that no one in that great crowd ever knew what happened later on that night.

*   *   *

WALKING ON THE WATER

For a moment, Jesus watched the crowd trailing home, back along the sandy lakeside path.

Out on the water, He could just see His disciples' boat, with its sail stiff in the breeze.

Then He turned to go higher up the mountain, to spend the evening in prayer.

"With this breeze, we shall soon be safely back," Peter said. "You others can rest. Andrew and I can handle the boat."

Just as he spoke, a rough gust of

wind suddenly pulled the rope from
Peter's hand.

Another gust blew from the other
side, and all the disciples fell in a heap
on the floor of the boat.

"Help me to get the sail down, there's a storm coming," Peter shouted above the wind, to Andrew. "We'll lose the sail if we're not careful."

Andrew and Peter tugged at the ropes and lowered the sail. James and John quickly took the oars and began to row.

From side to side the boat tossed. Andrew and Peter took two more oars.

They rowed hard, but they made no headway.

The tossing waves swept into the boat and soaked them.

The boat went first one way and then another in the gusts of wind.

"We are not getting any nearer the shore," groaned Matthew, who never liked being out in a boat.

Up on the mountain, Jesus felt the wind on His face. He knew that a storm had risen, and that His disciples were working hard at the oars, against the wind.

Between three o'clock and six o'clock in the morning, He began walking over the lake, towards them.

He heard Peter call out, "Keep rowing! We must not give up," and He saw the boat rising and falling in the big waves.

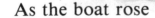

As the boat rose
on a wave, Peter saw Jesus coming
towards them. Another wave dashed
over the boat and hid Him from view.
The moon came out, and again Peter
saw Jesus. All the others saw Him too.

"A ghost! Did you see that ghost?"
one of them called.

They rowed on, terrified. Jesus
walked nearer and nearer.

"It is a ghost," the disciples
screamed.

Above the howling wind, they heard a voice call to them. They knew the voice. It was Jesus. They heard Him say, "Don't be afraid. It is I, Jesus."

"It is Jesus, walking towards us on the water, through the storm!" the disciples exclaimed.

Peter rested his oars, and called out loudly to Jesus, "Lord, if it really *is* you, tell me to come out to you on the water."

All the disciples listened for the answer. Was it really Jesus, or was it a ghost?

"Come to me!" Jesus' voice came clearly over the water.

Someone grabbed Peter's oars as he jumped over the side of the boat, on to the water. He began to walk over the waves, keeping his eyes all the time on Jesus, who was getting nearer and nearer.

The wind howled round Peter, and he could feel the waves tossing to and fro. He took his eyes off Jesus, and looked at the fierce splashing waves. He felt his feet sinking down, down into the water.

"Save me, Lord!" he shouted.

"Peter is sinking!" the disciples cried out in panic.

In one stride Jesus reached Peter, grabbed hold of him and pulled him to the surface.

"Why did you not trust me?" He asked. "Do you have so little faith?"

Together, Jesus and Peter climbed into the boat. The wind dropped and the waves became smooth.

All the disciples worshipped and praised Jesus joyfully.

"You really *are* the Son of God!" they cried out.